Lerner SPORTS

MUHAMMAD ALI

I AM THE GREATEST

PERCY LEED

LERNER PUBLICATIONS ◆ MINNEAPOLIS

Lerner Publications Company
An imprint of Lerner Publishing Group, Inc.
241 First Avenue North
Minneapolis, MN 55401 USA

For reading levels and more information, look up this title at www.lernerbooks.com.

Main body text set in Myriad Pro Semibold.
Typeface provided by Adobe.

Designer: Susan Fienhage

Library of Congress Cataloging-in-Publication Data

Names: Leed, Percy, 1968– author.
Title: Muhammad Ali : the champ / Joyce L. Hutchinson.
Description: Minneapolis : Lerner Publications, [2021] | Series: Epic sports bios | Includes bibliographical references and index. | Audience: Ages 7–11 | Audience: Grades 2–3 | Summary: "Muhammad Ali began boxing at age 12 to protect himself from bullies and became the heavyweight champion of the world three times. Learn about Ali's boxing career, his political activism, his biggest fights, and more"— Provided by publisher.
Identifiers: LCCN 2019058488 (print) | LCCN 2019058489 (ebook) | ISBN 9781541597426 (library binding) | ISBN 9781728413419 (paperback) | ISBN 9781728400105 (ebook)
Subjects: LCSH: Ali, Muhammad, 1942–2016—Juvenile literature. | Boxers (Sports)—United States—Biography—Juvenile literature.
Classification: LCC GV1132.A4 L44 2021 (print) | LCC GV1132.A4 (ebook) | DDC 796.83092 [B]—dc23

LC record available at https://lccn.loc.gov/2019058488
LC ebook record available at https://lccn.loc.gov/2019058489

Manufactured in the United States of America
1-47846-48286-12/17/2019

CONTENTS

HOMETOWN HERO

On September 5, 1960, a boxer from Louisville, Kentucky, stepped into a boxing ring in Rome, Italy. Muhammad Ali, known then as Cassius Clay, was fighting in the Summer Olympics. If he beat Zbigniew Pietrzykowski in the three-round match, Clay would win the gold medal.

Cassius Clay punches Gennadiy Shatkov in the 1960 Summer Olympics. Clay beat Shatkov and two other boxers to reach the gold medal match.

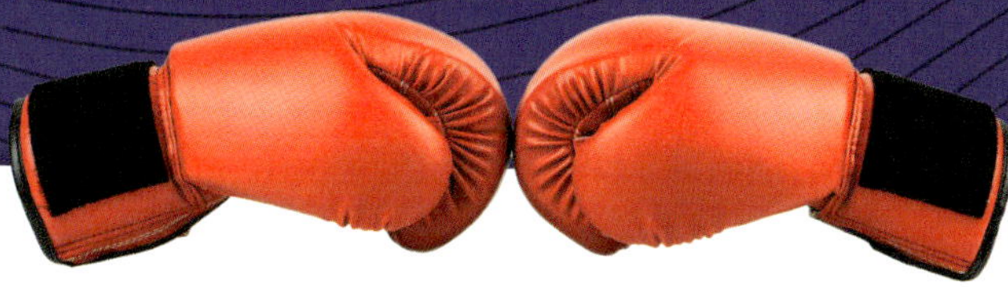

FACTS AT A GLANCE

Date of birth: January 17, 1942

League: pro boxing

Professional highlights: fought 61 pro boxing matches and lost just five times; won the heavyweight championship for the first time in 1964; won an Olympic gold medal in 1960

Personal highlights: began boxing at the age of 12; practiced boxing six days a week as a kid; lit the Olympic torch at the 1996 Olympic Games

The first round went badly for Clay. Pietrzykowski landed blow after blow. In the second round, Clay landed four hard punches on Pietrzykowski's head. By the third round, the older Pietrzykowski had begun to slow. Clay dazed him with a series of punches.

After the third round, Clay still looked fresh. But Pietrzykowski was tired and bleeding from cuts on his face. The fight's judges named Clay the winner.

The referee raises Clay's arm after the announcement that Clay won the fight.

Clay (*center*) wears his gold medal. The 1960 medals were the first Olympic medals designed to be worn around the neck.

Clay was so proud of his gold medal that he refused to take it off. He even slept with it. When he returned to Louisville, he received a hero's welcome. Less than two months later, Clay launched his pro career. He went on to rule the boxing world for two decades.

TOMORROW'S CHAMPION

Cassius Marcellus Clay Jr. was born in Louisville on January 17, 1942. He was named after Cassius Marcellus Clay, a farmer who owned slaves in Kentucky before the Civil War (1861–1865). Cassius's great-grandfather lived and worked as a freed slave on Clay's property. Like many freed slaves, Cassius's great-grandfather took the name of his white employer. The name had been passed down from father to son ever since.

Cassius learned to box to defend himself.

Columbia Gym is located on Louisville's Spalding University campus.

When he was 12, Cassius's parents bought him a new red-and-white bike. Two days later, the bike was stolen. Cassius was furious and began to cry.

Cassius, still crying, reported the crime to Joe Martin. Martin was a police officer who coached boxing at Columbia Gym. Cassius told Martin he wanted to fight the person who stole his bike. Martin listened patiently. Then he told Cassius that if he was going to make threats, he better learn to fight. The next night, Cassius went to Columbia Gym to begin learning to box.

Clay was loaded with boxing talent. He also trained harder than most boxers his age.

Six weeks later, Cassius made his TV boxing debut. Martin ran a local show called *Tomorrow's Champions*. Cassius stood 4 feet (1.2 m) tall. Like his opponent, he weighed 89 pounds (40 kg).

The two boys swung wildly at each other during the three-minute fight. Cassius landed a few more blows than his opponent landed, and the judges named him the winner. Cassius was thrilled. He shouted that he would soon be "the greatest of all time."

Cassius showed a natural talent for boxing. Just as important was his desire to succeed. As a teenager, he began training like a pro. He woke up early to run several

DIVIDED CITY

Unjust laws meant that Louisville was a segregated city when Cassius was growing up. People of color had to sit in the back of buses. They couldn't use the same public bathrooms white people used. Only certain theaters, hospitals, and schools were open to people of color.

miles before school. Six days a week, he worked out at the gym in the afternoon. Martin had never seen a young boxer work so hard.

Clay had an incredible amateur boxing record of 100–8. He wanted to turn pro in 1960. Instead, Martin convinced him to try out for the US Olympic team. Clay made the team and represented his country in the Olympics.

"THE KING OF THE WORLD"

Clay's Olympic gold medal was the last honor he would win as an amateur boxer. On October 29, 1960, he fought his first pro match in Louisville's Freedom Hall. His opponent was Tunney Hunsaker, a part-time fighter and full-time police chief.

Hunsaker, 29, had more experience than Clay had. Hunsaker had won 15 of his 20 pro fights. Yet Clay calmly

Clay strikes Hunsaker with a jab, a short straight blow.

beat him in six rounds. After the match, Hunsaker said Clay would "be heavyweight champion of the world someday."

Clay racked up pro wins with his unusual style. He used quick footwork and fast flurries of punches. He was big and strong, but he fought like a smaller, lighter boxer.

In November 1963, Clay agreed to fight Sonny Liston for the heavyweight championship of the world. Clay ranked as the top challenger for the title. Still, few boxing fans thought he could win. Liston was famous for his powerful punches. He usually beat his opponents in the early rounds. Some boxing experts thought Liston might hurt Clay so badly he would end Clay's career.

Clay leans away from Liston's punches. Liston knocked out 39 opponents in 54 career fights.

The fight took place on February 25, 1964. When the first round began, Clay moved quickly around the ring. He circled, stepped back, bobbed, weaved, and ducked. Liston punched and missed Clay badly. Again and again, Clay managed to slip away from Liston's punches.

In the third round, Clay changed his strategy. He had planned to save his strength for the fifth or sixth round, then fight hard once Liston had begun to tire. But Liston was slowing down already. Clay began to punch with more power.

Liston lowered his guard as he grew tired, leaving himself open to Clay's quick, powerful punches.

Clay celebrates with his training team after beating Liston.

By the sixth round, Clay had mostly stopped moving around the ring. Instead, he landed big punches on Liston. At one point, Clay hit Liston with eight straight punches. The crowd was in an uproar.

At the beginning of the seventh round, Clay bounced to his feet, ready to fight. Liston sat on his stool in the corner of the ring. He had given up. Clay raised both arms and danced across the ring. "I am the greatest," he shouted. "I'm the king of the world!"

WAR AND PROTEST

After winning the heavyweight championship, Clay announced that he had become a member of the Islamic faith. He changed his name to Muhammad Ali. He said his old name had come from a system of slavery, while his new name meant "beloved of God."

Ali talks about his name change in 1964. He insisted that people call him by his new name, but many newspapers continued to refer to him as Cassius Clay.

Ali began training again in the summer of 1964 for a rematch with Liston in November. Midway through the first round, Liston punched with his left hand. Ali jerked his chin back to avoid a hit. Then he punched Liston's head on the side. The punch was so quick that most fans didn't see it. Liston sank to his knees, then his elbow, and finally rolled onto his back. The fight was over less than two minutes after it began.

ROUND AND ROUND

The number of rounds in a pro boxing match varies. Fights may be as short as four rounds. When Ali first turned pro, championship fights were 15 rounds. To cut down on injuries, championship fights became 12 rounds in the 1980s.

In 1965, the United States entered the Vietnam War (1957–1975). The US government drafted many young people to serve in the armed forces. Ali was drafted, but he refused to go to war. He said he was a religious man of peace. Ignoring the draft was against the law. In June 1967, a jury found him guilty of refusing to serve.

Though Ali didn't go to jail, no state would allow him to box. He was stripped of his world championship title. For three and a half years, he was completely locked out of pro boxing. Instead, he began to speak at colleges around the country. Ali spoke about his religious and political beliefs and read poetry that he'd written.

Ali reads a newspaper with friends in 1966. The headline describes large US protests against the war in Vietnam.

Ali lands a blow to Jerry Quarry's face.

By 1970, public opinion in the United States had turned against the Vietnam War. To black communities and to young people, Ali had long been a symbol of peaceful protest. Many other Americans came to share their view. To them, Ali was a hero who had given up his career, his title, and millions of dollars in lost prize money for his beliefs.

Ali returned to the ring in October 1970. He beat Jerry Quarry in three rounds. Less than two months later, he beat Oscar Bonavena in 15 rounds. Ali was slower and tired more quickly than he had before his break from boxing. But he wanted to reclaim the heavyweight title as soon as possible. On March 8, 1971, he got his chance.

THE GREATEST

Ali faced Joe Frazier in the title fight. Frazier was a gold medalist at the 1964 Tokyo Olympics. He hadn't lost a fight in six years.

Joe Frazier (*left*) was one of the hardest punchers in boxing history. He knocked out Jimmy Ellis in the fourth round of this 1970 fight.

Sweat flies off Ali's head as Frazier connects with a big punch.

At times during the match, Ali looked like his old self. In the ninth round, he danced around Frazier. Then, in the 11th round, Frazier hit Ali with a powerful hook punch.

Ali's head snapped back, and his legs wobbled. Frazier landed another hook, and Ali barely stayed on his feet. The judges announced Frazier as the winner. It was the first loss of Ali's pro career.

Ali got another chance to win the title on October 30, 1974. The fight against George Foreman was called the Rumble in the Jungle. It took place in Kinshasa, Zaire (later named the Democratic Republic of the Congo), in Africa.

Ali spent most of the fight dodging big punches from Foreman. But Ali hit back too. In the eighth round, he sent a flurry of punches at Foreman and knocked him out. Ali was again the heavyweight champion of the world—10 years after he'd first won the title.

About 60,000 boxing fans attended the Rumble in the Jungle.

Ali was almost 40 years old when he fought Trevor Berbick.

By 1981, Ali had fought 60 pro matches. His body had taken a beating. On December 11, he fought Trevor Berbick in Nassau, Bahamas. Berbick was an average boxer, but he easily won the match. It was the last fight of Ali's career.

In September 1984, Ali checked into a hospital. He complained of slurred speech, trembling in his hands, and feeling tired. Doctors told him he had Parkinson's disease.

The illness robbed Ali of his most famous qualities. Once he had recited poetry, but the disease made it difficult to speak. Once he moved with grace and speed, but the disease made him slow and at risk of falling. His left hand, which threw thousands of powerful punches, shook almost all the time.

Ali speaks with reporters at a hospital in September 1984 after announcing that he has Parkinson's disease.

Sports fans around the world were thrilled to see Ali at the 1996 Olympics.

Despite his disease, Ali traveled the world and raised millions of dollars for charity. He appeared at the 1996 Olympic Games in Atlanta, Georgia. When he stepped onto the platform to light the Olympic flame and open the games, the crowd went wild.

In November 2005, the Muhammad Ali Center opened in Louisville. The center is dedicated to Ali's life. Exhibits highlight his training, his fights, and his experience at the 1996 Olympics.

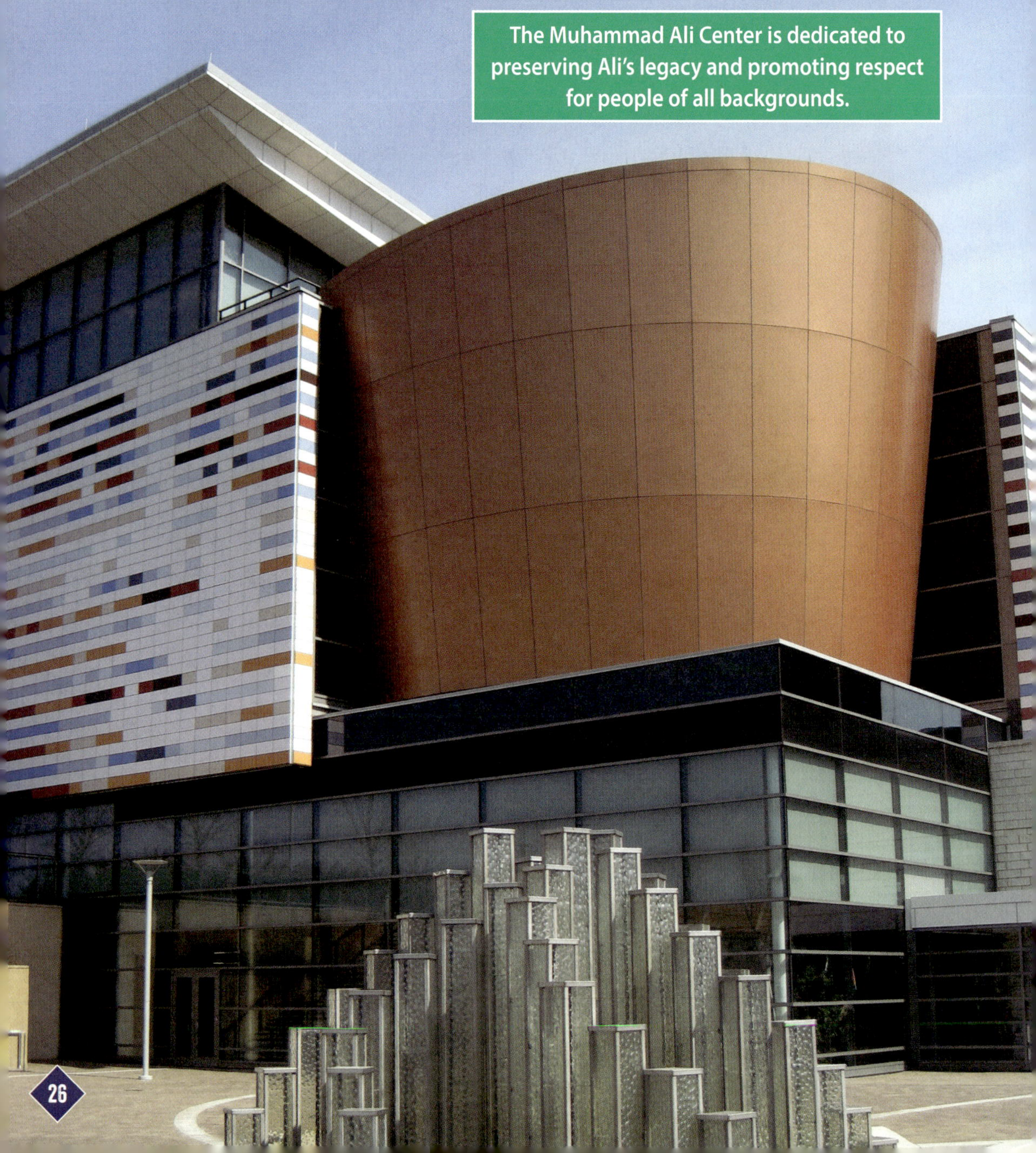

The Muhammad Ali Center is dedicated to preserving Ali's legacy and promoting respect for people of all backgrounds.

Ali signed this robe after the Rumble in the Jungle.

In June 2016, Ali died at the age of 74. But his legacy and impact on the sports world lives on. "In the history of the world from the beginning of time, there's never been another fighter like me," Ali said.

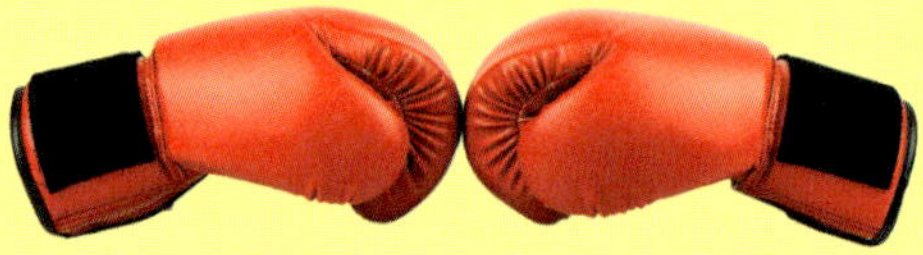

SELECTED FIGHT RECORD

October 29, 1960	**Tunney Hunsaker**	Win 1–0
February 25, 1964	**Sonny Liston**	Win 20–0
May 25, 1965	**Sonny Liston**	Win 21–0
November 22, 1965	**Floyd Patterson**	Win 22–0
March 8, 1971	**Joe Frazier**	Loss 31–1
September 20, 1972	**Floyd Patterson**	Win 39–1
March 31, 1973	**Ken Norton**	Loss 41–2
September 10, 1973	**Ken Norton**	Win 42–2
January 28, 1974	**Joe Frazier**	Win 44–2
October 30, 1974	**George Foreman**	Win 45–2
October 1, 1975	**Joe Frazier**	Win 49–2
September 28, 1976	**Ken Norton**	Win 53–2
February 15, 1978	**Leon Spinks**	Loss 55–3
September 15, 1978	**Leon Spinks**	Win 56–3
December 11, 1981	**Trevor Berbick**	Loss 56–5

GLOSSARY

amateur: someone who is not paid for an activity

debut: a first appearance

draft: required by the government to serve in the military

footwork: the movement of the feet

hook: a punch coming from the side of the body instead of going straight forward

judge: an official who scores each round of a boxing match

pro: people who are paid to play or compete in a sport

recite: to repeat from memory or read aloud in public

segregated: restricted to members of one group or one race

SOURCE NOTES

10 David Remnick, *King of the World* (New York: Random House, 1998), 92.

13 Thomas Hauser, *Muhammad Ali: His Life and Times* (New York: Simon & Schuster, 1991), 31.

15 Neil Steinberg, "Muhammad Ali, 'King of the World,' Dies at 74," *Chicago Sun-Times*, June 5, 2016, https://chicago.suntimes.com/2016/6/5/18365807/muhammad-ali-king-of-the-world-dies-at-74.

16 Alexandra Sims, "Muhammad Ali: Why Did the Boxing Legend Change His Name from Cassius Clay?," *Independent* (London), June 4, 2016, https://www.independent.co.uk/news/people/muhammad-ali-death-cassius-clay-why-did-he-change-his-name-nation-of-islam-a7065256.html.

27 Hauser, *Muhammad Ali*, 462.

FURTHER INFORMATION

Braun, Eric. *The Civil Rights Movement*. Minneapolis: Lerner Publications, 2019.

Doeden, Matt. *Muhammad Ali: The Greatest*. Minneapolis: Lerner Publications, 2017.

The Legacy of Muhammad Ali
http://kpcnotebook.scholastic.com/post/legacy-muhammad-ali

Llana, Sheila Griffin. *Children in the Civil Rights Era*. Lake Elmo, MN: Focus Readers, 2019.

Muhammad Ali
https://www.ducksters.com/biography/athletes/muhammad_ali.php

Muhammad Ali Center
https://alicenter.org/

INDEX

PHOTO ACKNOWLEDGMENTS

Image credits: Popperfoto/Getty Images, p. 4; Woraphon Nusen/EyeEm/Getty Images, pp. 5, 28; Wikimedia Commons (public domain), p. 6; FPG/Archive Photos/Getty Images, p. 7; Bettmann/Getty Images, pp. 8, 10, 12, 15, 18, 24; BRENDAN SMIALOWSKI/AFP/Getty Images, p. 9; Tony Triolo/Focus of Sport/Getty Images, p. 13; Herb Scharfman/The LIFE Images Collection/Getty Images, pp. 14, 16; JARNOUX Patrick/Paris Match/Getty Images, p. 19; Rolls Press/Popperfoto/Getty Images, p. 20; Dick Morseman/Newsday LLC/Getty Images, p. 21; STR/AFP/Getty Images, p. 22; Focus on Sport/Getty Images, p. 23; Michael Cooper/Getty Images, p. 25; local louisville/flickr (CC BY 2.0), p. 26; Jerod Harris/Getty Images, p. 27. Design element throughout: saicle/iStock/Getty Images.

Cover: Stanley Weston Archive/Getty Images (portrait); Bettmann/Getty Images (background).